# Tricky Fox Tales



Chris Schweizer

Illustrated by
Shelli Paroline

Graphic Universe™ • Minneapolis • New York

Story by Chris Schweizer

Pencils and inks by Shelli Paroline

Coloring by John Novak

Lettering by Grace Lu



Graphic Universe™
A division of Lerner Publishing Group, Inc.
241 First Avenue North
Minneapolis, MN 55401 U.S.A.

Website address: www.lernerbooks.com

Library of Congress Cataloging-in-Publication Data

Schweizer, Chris.
Tricky Fox tales / by Chris Schweizer ; illustrated by Shelli Paroline.
p. cm. — (Tricky journeys)
Summary: Fox tries to stop her cousin Roxy from acting like a bully, and the reader helps her make choices as they encounters many other creatures, some friendly and some dangerous.
ISBN 978–0–7613–6605–8 (lib. bdg. : alk. paper)
1. Plot-your-own stories. 2. Graphic novels. [1. Graphic novels. 2. Foxes—Fiction. 3. Tricksters—Fiction. 4. Animals—Fiction. 5. Plot-your-own stories.] I. Paroline, Shelli, ill. II. Title.
PZ7.7.S39Tqf 2011
741.5'973—dc22 2010050902

Manufactured in the United States of America
1 – CG – 7/15/11

Are you ready for
your Tricky Journeys™?

You'll find yourself right smack
in the middle of this story's tricks,
jokes, thrills, and fun.

Each page tells what happens to Fox
and her friends. **YOU** get to decide
what happens next. Read each page
until you reach a choice. Then pick the
choice **YOU** like best.

But be careful . . . one wrong
choice could land Fox in a
mess even she can't trick
her way out of!

Fox loves going to the marketplace. The merchants have goods from all over the world. An old crane is selling pretty beads.

Fox is looking at the beads when a mink crashes into her! They tumble down and knock the old crane's table over. Jewelry scatters everywhere.

"Hey!" says Fox. "Why don't you watch where you're going?"

"It's not my fault," the mink says. He points. "Look!"

 Go on to the next page.

Go on to the next page.

Fox used to play with Roxy every day. Roxy used to be so nice! Maybe there's a reason she's acting so mean. Fox could talk to her about it.

Then again, sometimes bullies need to be taught a lesson, or they'll keep being bullies. Fox could play a trick on her!

If Fox tries to talk Roxy into being nicer,

TURN TO PAGE 46.

If Fox tries to trick Roxy,

TURN TO PAGE 30.

Go on to the next page.

Fox is terrified. The kappa wants to eat them!

If Fox is polite to the kappa,

TURN TO PAGE 24.

If Fox unties Roxy so that they can fight the kappa,

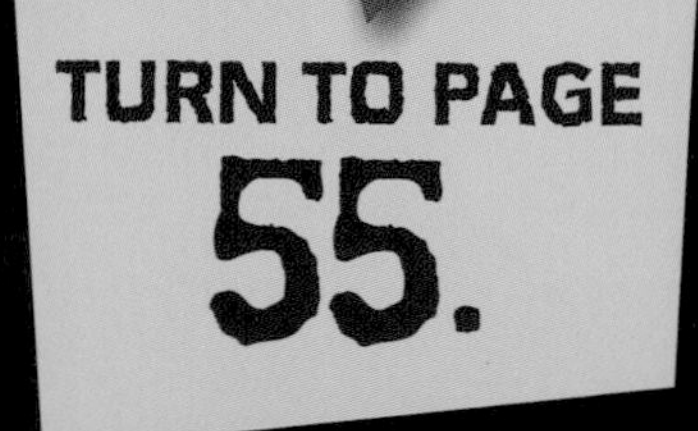

"I accept," says Fox. "I'll untie you."

"No need," says Roxy. She flexes her muscles. With a POP POP POP, the ropes snap and fall to the ground.

Fox shakes her head. "You may be strong, but I'm quick, and I use my head!"

"I'll use your head to ring the town bell!" Roxy says.

Fox hops into the air as Roxy kicks at her with her big feet. She ducks as Roxy swipes at her with her big claws. Roxy smashes one of the marketplace tables.

"If I don't move the fight away from here, there won't be any market left!" thinks Fox.

Go on to the next page.

"Maybe I can get Roxy to follow me to the beach," thinks Fox. "But if we go into the woods, it will be easier for me to hide!"

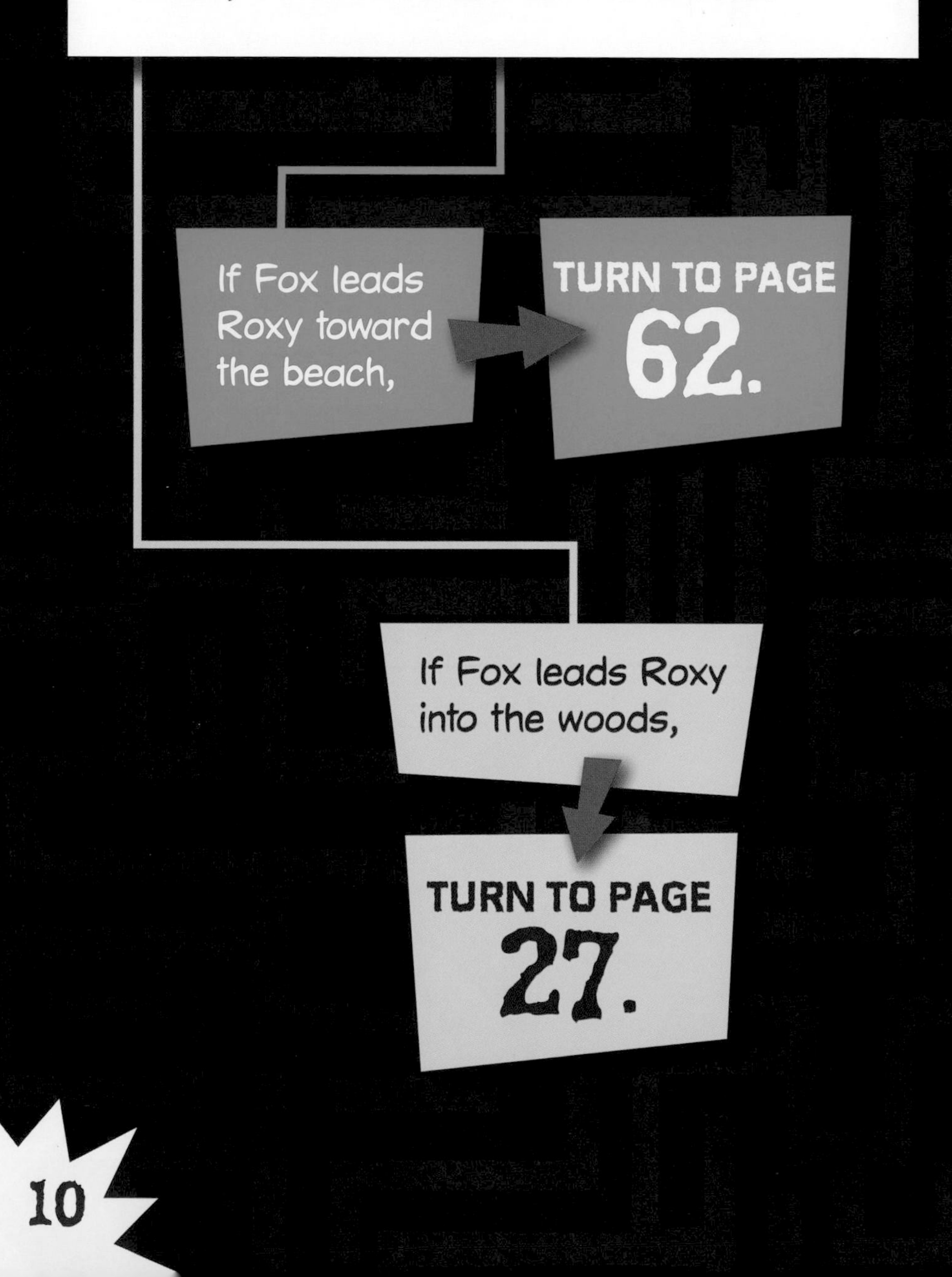

"Here's what we'll do," Fox says to Roxy. "I'll say that I'm you, and you'll say that you're me!"

"So we won't have any disguises at all?" asks Roxy.

"No," says Fox. "It's a trick!"

"Oh!" says Roxy, clapping her hands. "I love a good trick!"

Suddenly two little turtles come running by. "Did you hear about Tanuki's disguise?" asks one.

"What is it?" asks the other.

"He is disguised as the emperor! He has one hundred bodyguards walking beside him!"

Go on to the next page. 

"That's the best disguise I've ever seen!" says Roxy.

"You haven't seen it yet," says Fox. But it sounds as if Fox has no chance of winning.

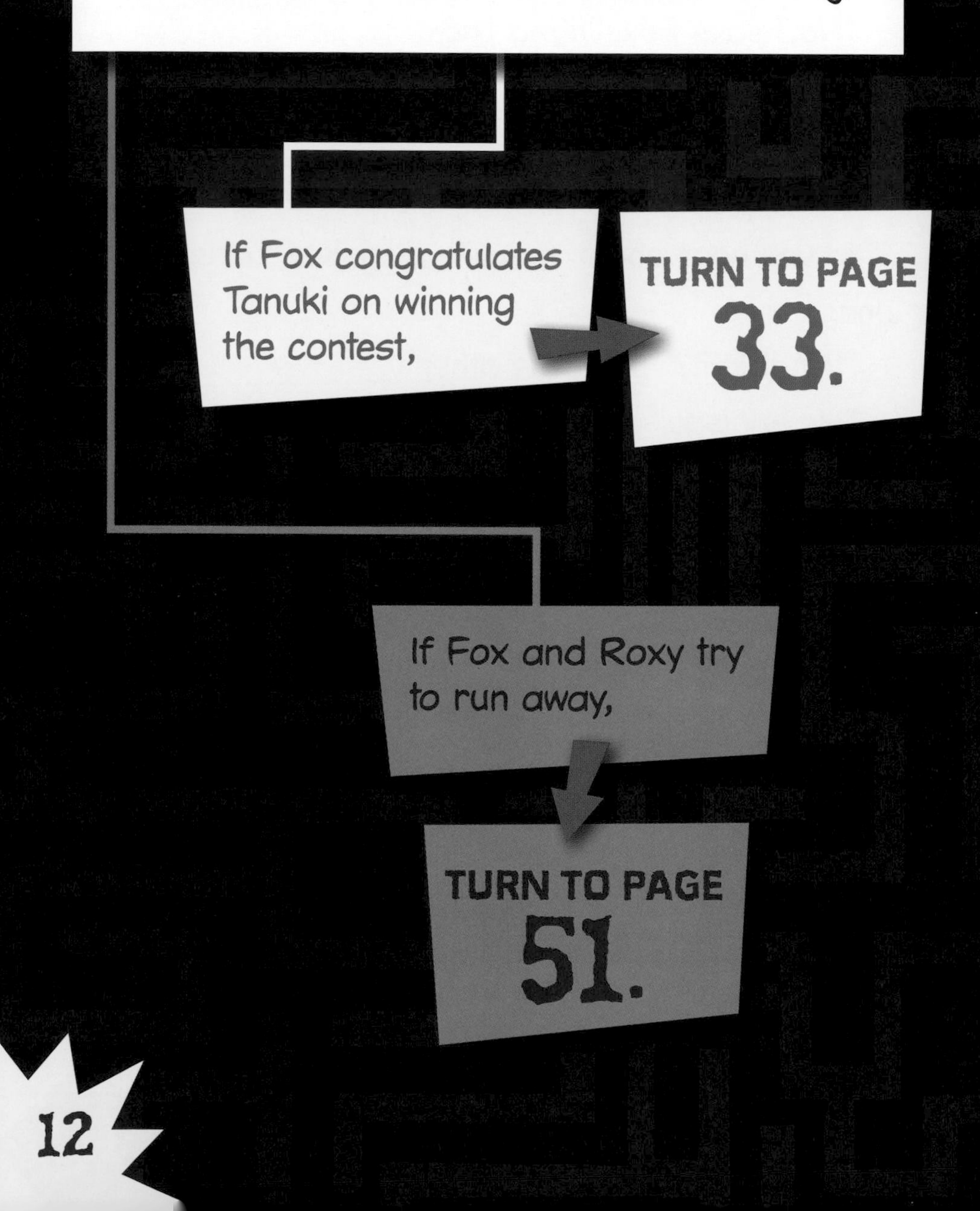

If Fox congratulates Tanuki on winning the contest,

TURN TO PAGE 33.

If Fox and Roxy try to run away,

TURN TO PAGE 51.

"It's oysters that you owe him, so it's oysters you should give him," says Fox. "Let's go dig them up while the tide's out."

Many hours later, Fox and Roxy are still digging. They only have half a basket. It'll be many days before they dig up enough oysters to repay Otter. Roxy looks happy, though. She's glad to be done with bullying.

Fox is not so happy! She sighs. This may fix her family's reputation, but it's hard on her back!

**THE END**

Hold still, you varmint!
Hey!
You won't be putting ANYONE in this bag, Tanuki!
Give me back that bag!
No way! I just took it FROM you!
But it's a MAGIC bag.
I have to HOLD ONTO it, or...
AAAAH!

Thugs, goons, and monsters fall all around Fox. There are dozens of them.

"I have to hold onto it, or every bad creature I've ever captured will get free!" cries Tanuki. "The bag was a prison. Now we have to stop these guys from causing trouble again!"

Go on to the next page. 

Tanuki captured all these creeps before. But maybe he's outmatched now. Fox wonders if she can catch them all herself.

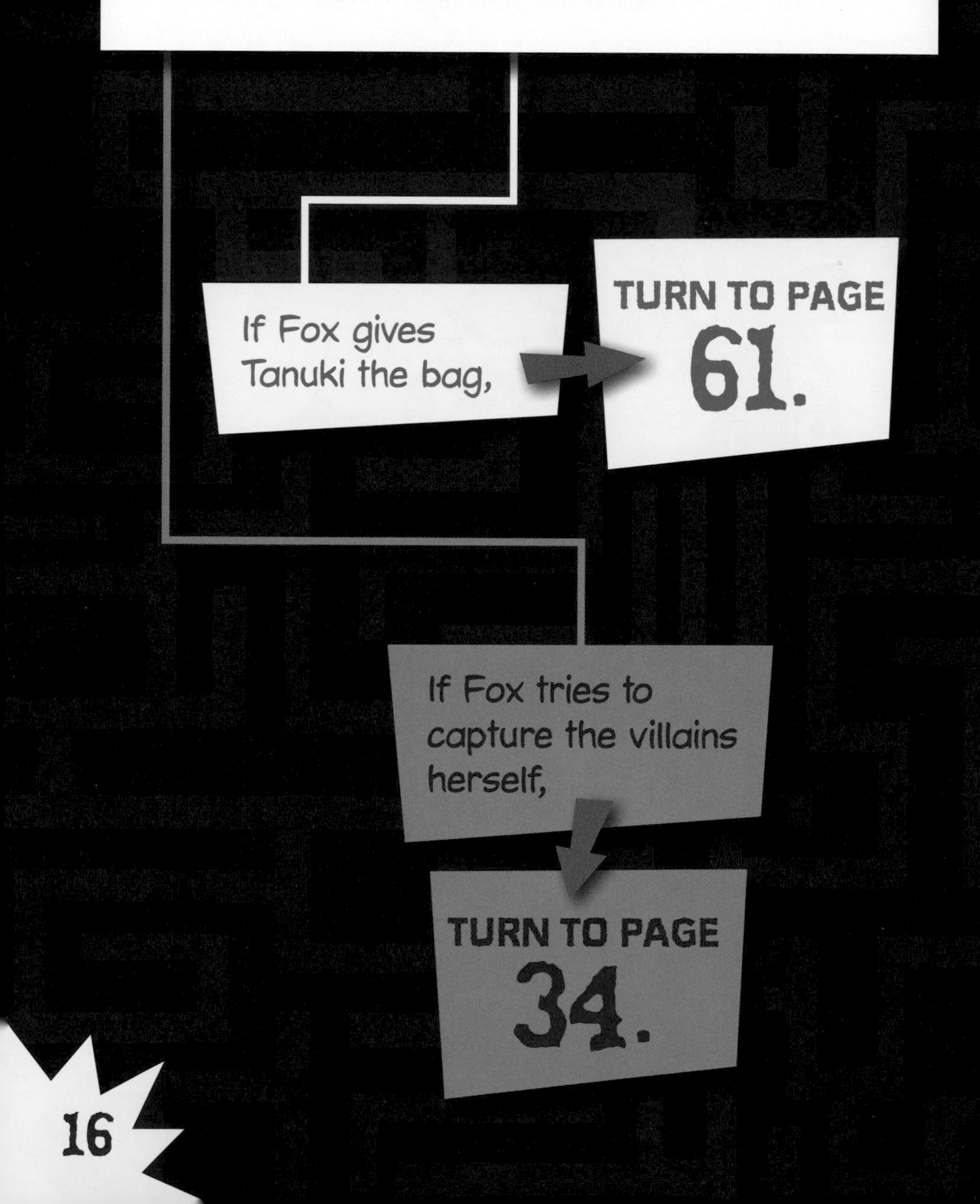

"Excuse me, sir," says Fox to the old fellow in the gold robes. "If you are as rich as you look, you need a pair of fine bodyguards!"

The old gentleman laughs. "I'm not rich!" he says. "This is a costume! I'm an actor in the opera. But if you're looking for work, we need curtain pullers to open and close the curtains during the show."

"That sounds good!" says Roxy. "I didn't like the idea of getting into fights as a bodyguard. I'm not a bully anymore."

"It's a deal," says Fox.

They all walk to the theater, dancing as the actor sings a beautiful song.

**THE END**

 Go on to the next page.

"I warned you!" says the umbrella. The other yokai hop and roll toward Fox.

"Leave my cousin alone!" Roxy says. She swats a flying lamp. A boot with hair kicks her. Fox is knocked down. Soon both Roxy and Fox are caught!

"Now," says the umbrella, "you must work for us . . . FOREVER! Or we'll hold you down until you waste away."

Fox and Roxy agree to be the yokai's servants. It's either that or this will be

***THE END***

"You can't fit a big fox like Roxy in a tiny bag like that!" says Fox.

Tanuki sticks out his tongue at Fox. He jumps into the air with the bag over his head. It puffs up like a parachute and grows bigger and bigger. Tanuki drops the bag over Roxy's head and scoops the bag up. Roxy is gone!

"How did you do that?" asks Fox.

"It's a magic bag," says Tanuki. "Now I'm coming after you!"

"Tanuki is dangerous!" thinks Fox. "I don't want to leave my cousin behind, but I don't want to be trapped in that bag, either!"

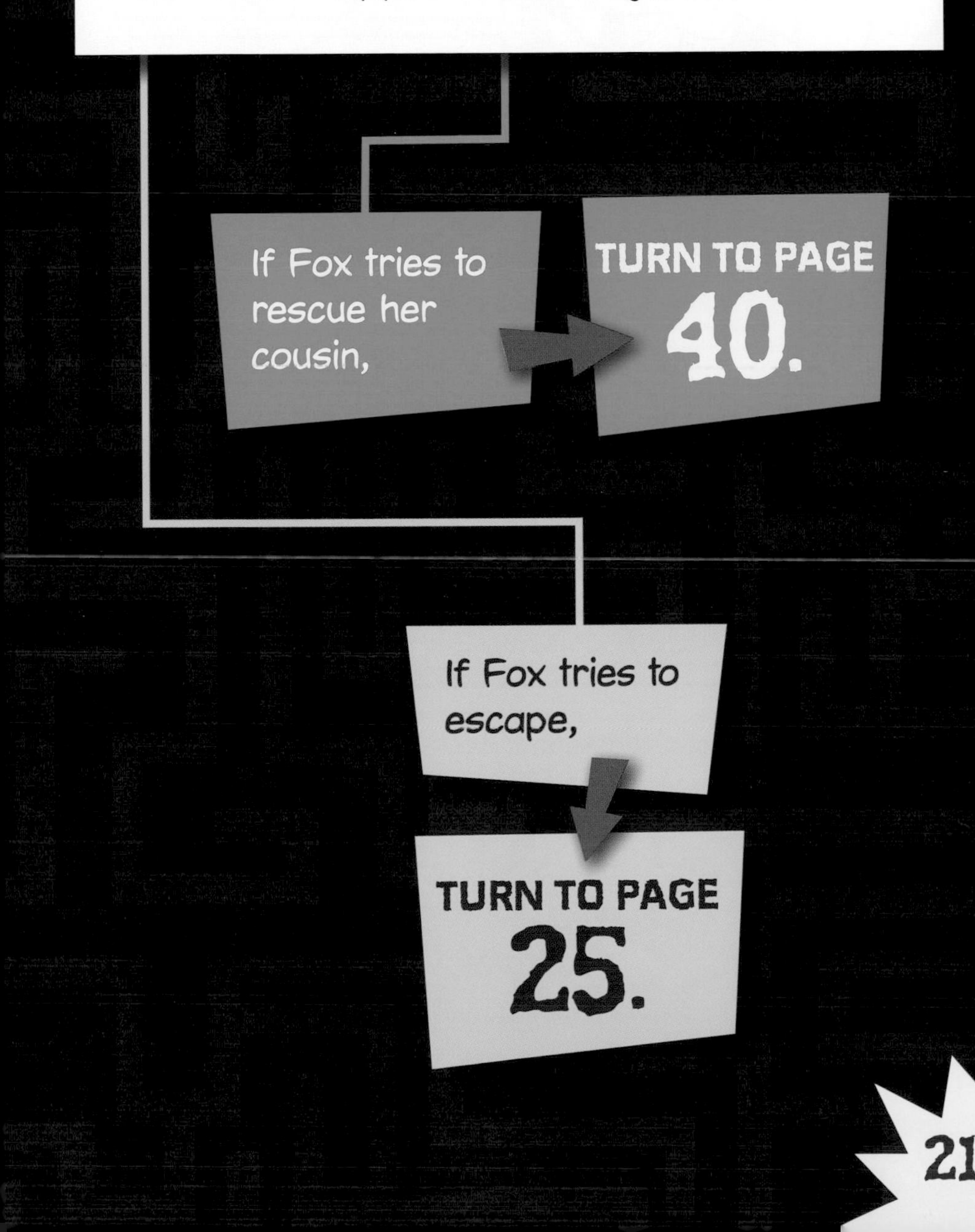

If Fox tries to rescue her cousin,

TURN TO PAGE 40.

If Fox tries to escape,

TURN TO PAGE 25.

Go on to the next page.

"That's a lot of oysters," says Roxy. "How will I ever be able to repay him?"

If Fox suggests that they gather oysters for Otter,

TURN TO PAGE 13.

If Fox suggests that they get jobs so they can pay back Otter,

TURN TO PAGE 59.

"Forgive us for being so rude, Kappa," says Fox, bowing low.

"I love a polite meal!" says the kappa. It bows too, and all the water pours out of the bowl in its head. It falls down with a PLOP on the riverbank.

"What happened?" asks Fox.

"Kappas can't stay awake if there's no water in their heads!" says Roxy. "It'll sleep until rain fills its head back up."

Fox makes Roxy promise not to be a bully anymore. They follow the floating cucumbers and row home as fast as they can!

You won't get ME!
Of COURSE I will! I NEVER let a DANGER to this village escape!
I was trying to help!
NOW you're trying to TRICK me!
NO ONE tricks TANUKI.
Any last words before I put you away for GOOD, trickster?
Go on to the next page.

For once, Fox is at a loss for words. She opens her mouth, but only a squeak comes out. Tanuki stuffs her into the bag. Fox feels herself falling, falling, falling. It's a magic bag, and she is going to fall for a very long time.

When she does finally stop, only then will it be

# THE END

You can run, but I´ll catch you!
I´m so small, I can dart around these trees. Roxy is so big, she will have to move slowly!
Then again, I could be WRONG!
I´ve got you now!
Maybe you DO . . .
. . . and maybe you DON´T!
SCRUNCH

Roxy struggles, but she's stuck tight. "Help me!" yells Roxy. "I'm sorry I was mean. Please let me out!" She starts to cry.

Maybe Roxy really is sorry, but maybe she's trying to trick Fox!

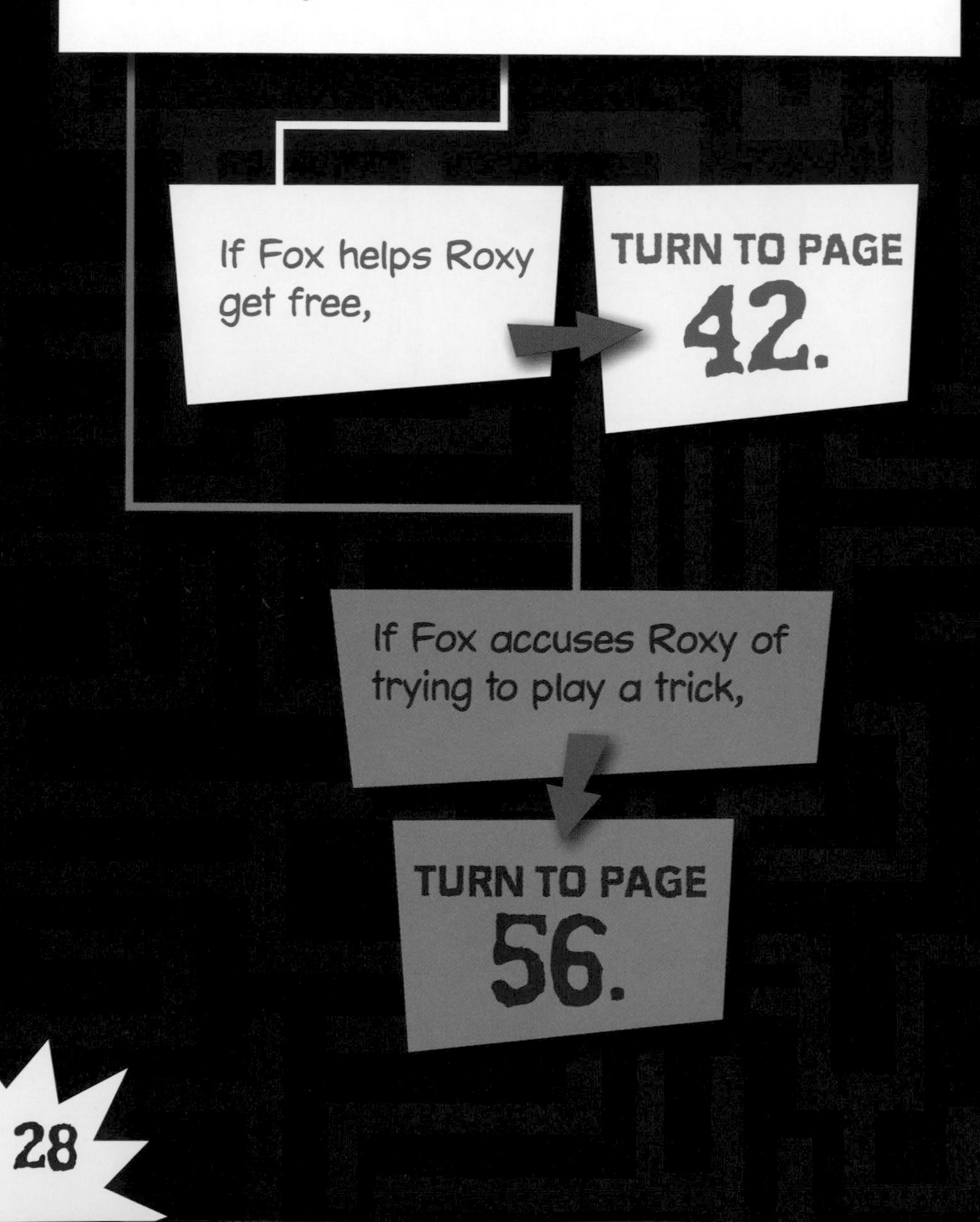

If Fox helps Roxy get free,

TURN TO PAGE 42.

If Fox accuses Roxy of trying to play a trick,

TURN TO PAGE 56.

"Out you go," says Fox, pushing Roxy to the side of the boat.

"Wait!" yells Roxy. "Untie me first, or I'll sink!"

Fox unties her cousin. As soon as Roxy is free, she grabs Fox and throws her over the treetops and into the swamp.

"So long!" Fox hears Roxy say, but she can't tell where the voice is coming from. Fox runs one way. Then she runs another. She's stuck in the swamp and will NEVER find her way out again. For her, this is

**THE END**

"Talking to Roxy won't do any good," Fox says to herself. "But I know what will!"

Fox goes to Otter, who runs the oyster stand. "Otter!" says Fox. "Does that big fox push you around?"

"Every day!" says Otter, tears in his eyes. "She takes all my oysters. If this keeps up, I'll lose my shop!"

"Maybe we can trick her so she won't try to take your oysters again," Fox says, reaching out her paw. "Now hand me your cape and hat!"

Hey, oyster otter! I'm ready for my oysters!
Oh, by all means! Eat your fill.
You look SHORTER.
Ha, ha! Everyone looks short to you! Now eat up!
She's so wrapped up in tasting the oysters that she doesn't notice the ropes!
SLURP!
Delicious, delicious, delicious!
Go on to the next page.

"I'm full," says Roxy. "But I can't just leave all these oysters, can I?" She gives a mean laugh and reaches for the basket. Only then does she realize that she's all tied up!

"Hey," Roxy yells, "let me go!"

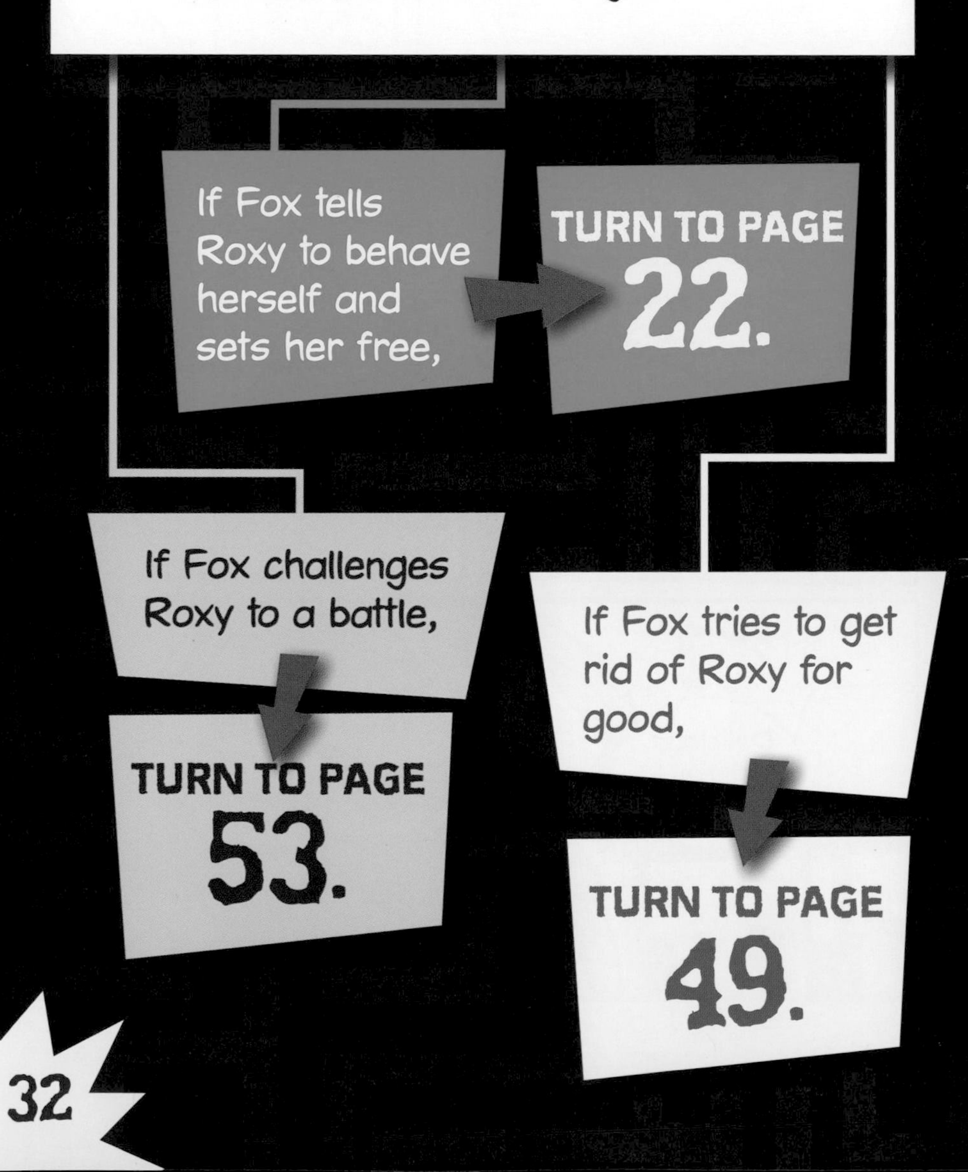

Fox and Roxy go to see the emperor's parade. "That IS the best disguise I've ever seen!" exclaims Fox.

"Oh, Tanuki!" she yells. "What a wonderful disguise!"

"How dare you yell at the emperor!" yells a bodyguard, hitting Fox on the head with a piece of bamboo.

"How dare you interrupt the emperor's parade!" yells another. He also whacks Fox on the head.

Fox sees Tanuki hiding in the weeds with the two little turtles. Too late, Fox realizes that this is the REAL emperor! This time Fox is the one who was tricked!

Go on to the next page.

"I'll help you," says Fox. "I have a magic bag too." She holds up Tanuki's bag. "Everyone climb inside, and I'll take you to safety!"

"Get back!" she yells to Tanuki. "I won't let you capture these creatures again!"

"She's tough!" says a monster. He dives into the bag.

"This fox will keep us safe!" says another monster. He dives into the bag too. The others follow him in.

"Thanks!" says Tanuki. "I never could have captured them again. We should team up!"

"Sounds great!" says Fox.

Fox, Roxy, and Tanuki laugh, glad that the danger has reached

# THE END

"I'll leave you tied up," says Fox. "You're not getting this umbrella!" She turns around and starts to walk away. Then she hears a snap. And another snap. Roxy is breaking the ropes!

"Did you think rope could hold me?" asks Roxy. "I'm the strongest animal in the country!"

Fox tries to get away, but Roxy catches her. "My umbrella!" cries Fox as Roxy plucks it from her hands.

"You mean MY umbrella," says Roxy. She grabs Fox and throws her all the way to

## THE END

Psshh! Imagine someone else thinking he is a "master of disguise."
Everyone knows that I'M the best at disguises in the whole country.
THAT'S NOT TRUE!
I'M the best!
There's only one way to settle this . . .
A DISGUISE CONTEST!
May the best disguise win!
Yeah, MINE!
What is he doing?

"He's leaving a biscuit at the statue of the lucky monkey," replies Fox. "Legend says it will give him good luck. But I have the perfect idea for this contest!"

"I had no idea you were alive," says Fox. "I thought you were just a gift from my great-grandma. I'm sorry that I kept you against your will."

"I wasn't alive until just now," says the umbrella. "I am grateful to you for treating your great-grandma's gift so well. My name is Karakasa, and I can grant you one wish."

Fox and Roxy look at each other with wide grins. Usually, Fox feels as if she has only one or two choices. But this time, the possibilities are endless! Whatever she decides, for now this is...

## THE END

My cousin WAS being a bully, and that's not right . . .
. . . but trapping her in a magic bag is NOT the way to teach her to be nice!
I don't care about teaching her a LESSON.
The villagers pay me to catch troublemakers.
I have a REPUTATION to maintain!
So you don't even care about doing the right thing!
I guess there's no talking with you. I should just let you throw the bag over my head.
Good! I HATE it when I have to WORK HARD!

Tanuki starts to swing the bag over Fox . . . but Fox snatches it out of his hands!

"My bag!" Tanuki yells. "Give it back!"

"Not until I let out everyone you trapped!" says Fox. She turns the bag over and shakes it. First, Roxy falls out, then a duck. Then an octopus, a few monsters, and a bear.

"Should we throw this raccoon dog into his own bag?" asks Fox.

The animals all nod yes. Tanuki gulps. He knows that for him, this is

**THE END**

"Poor Roxy," thinks Fox. "She's big, but she's still a kid like me!"

"Please get me out!" begs Roxy, tears rolling down her cheeks.

Fox pushes the tip of her umbrella between Roxy and the tree trunk and pulls on it. With a squeak, Roxy pops free.

"Thanks," Roxy starts to say, but then she stops. The umbrella is glowing!

The umbrella shoots out of Fox's hands, opens up, and gives a big groan. Eyes appear. "Woooo-EEEE!" it screams.

"My umbrella!" yells Fox.

 Go on to the next page.

"I'm not anybody's ANYTHING anymore!" howls the umbrella. "I just turned one hundred years old. That means I get to be a YOKAI if I want to! And I want to! No more keeping people dry for me, no sir!" It hops up and down on its handle.

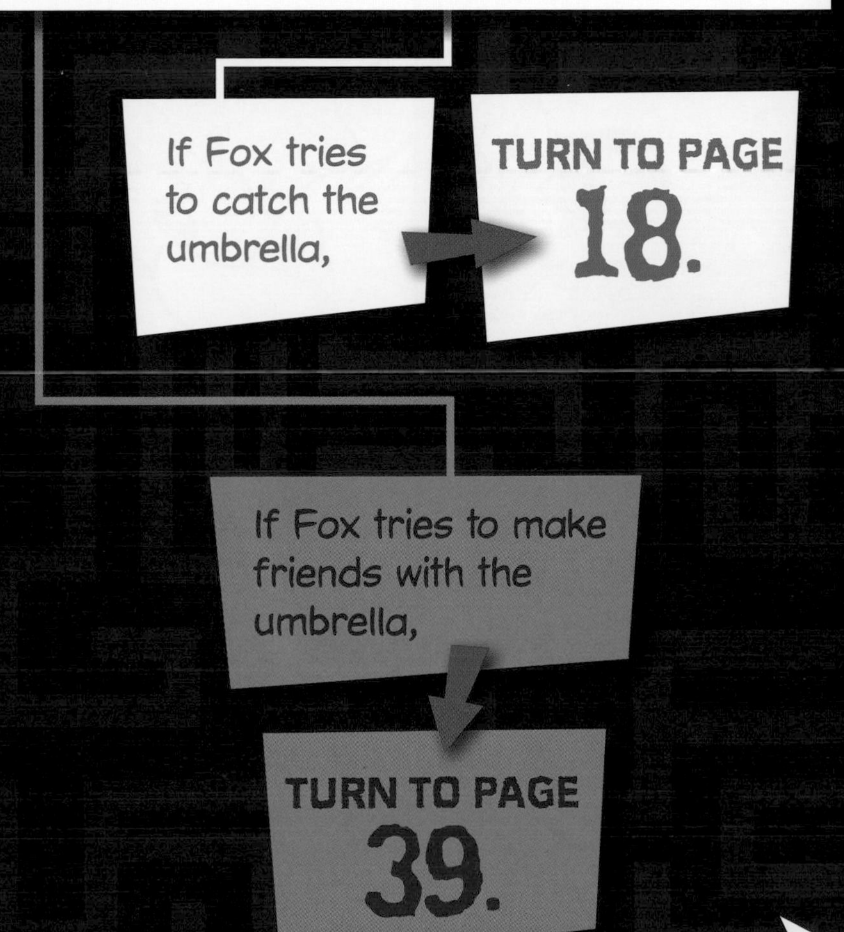

If Fox tries to catch the umbrella, TURN TO PAGE 18.

If Fox tries to make friends with the umbrella, TURN TO PAGE 39.

Go on to the next page.

"Maybe they want to rob you themselves," says Little One-Inch.

"That's not true," says Fox, but Little One-Inch pokes her in the nose with his tiny sword. "Yow!" howls Fox.

Little One-Inch jumps into the air and pokes Roxy in the paw. "Ouch!" cries Roxy.

The two foxes take off running. Little One-Inch jumps from one to the other, jabbing them with his very tiny but very sharp little sword.

Oh, how Fox wishes this would hurry up and come to

 Go on to the next page.

"Easy, Tanuki," says Fox. "I have this under control. Roxy here was just leaving."

Tanuki swings his club at Fox. Fox jumps out of the way. "Leaving isn't good enough!" he says. He swings again. "You foxes think you're so clever, but you're not as clever as I am! I'm a master of disguise. I'm going to put that big bully in this bag!"

Roxy laughs. "I'll never fit in that bag!" she says.

Go on to the next page.

Fox isn't sure what she should do. Tanuki's bag is much smaller than Roxy. Can Tanuki really put Roxy in it? Fox is pretty good at disguises herself, so maybe she can hurt Tanuki's pride!

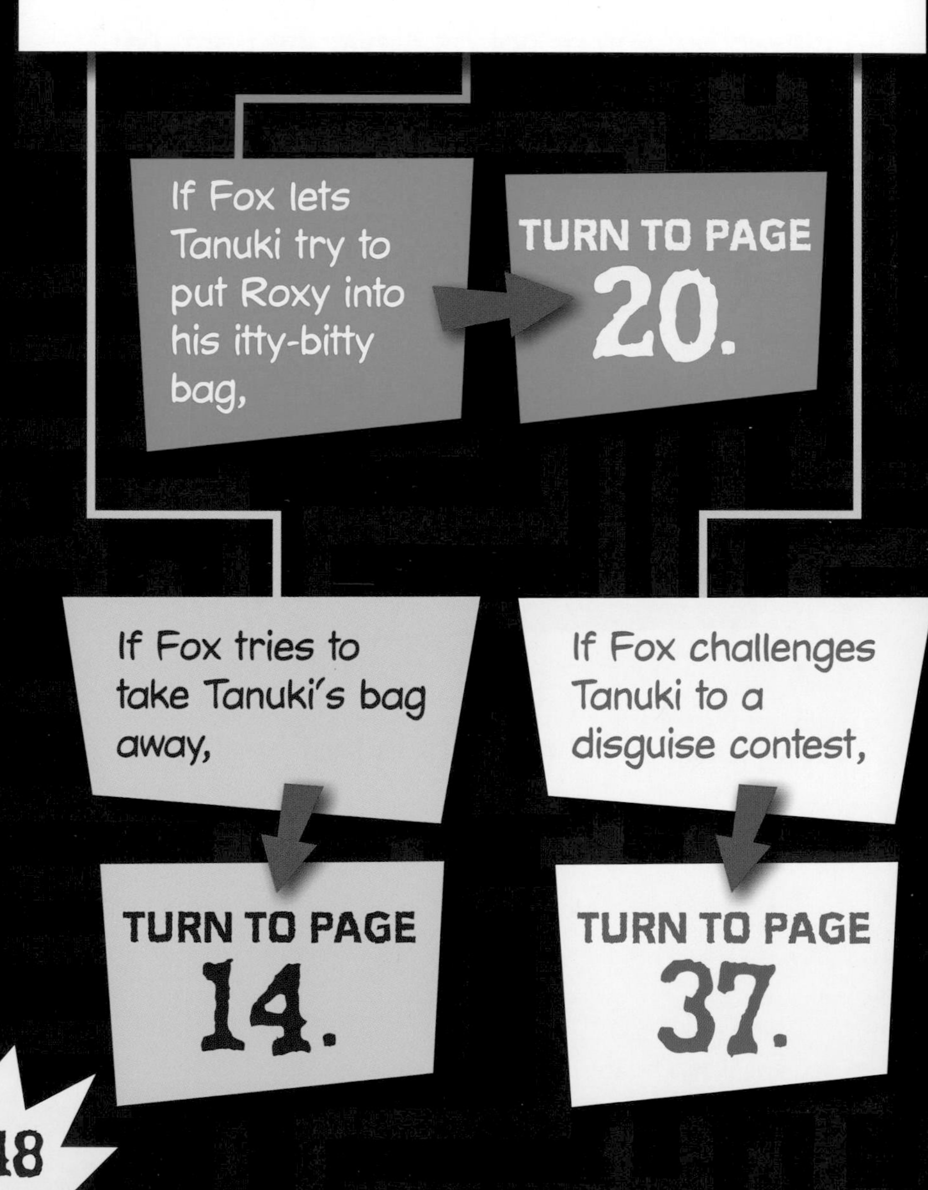

Go on to the next page.

Fox steers the boat for hours, until they get to the edge of the swamp. Fox is nervous. She doesn't want to go too far in, but she has to make sure that Roxy can't get out!

If Fox dumps Roxy into the water right here,

TURN TO PAGE 29.

If Fox takes Roxy into the swamp and dumps her out on land,

TURN TO PAGE 7.

Go on to the next page. 

Fox tries to run, but she is grabbed by one of the bodyguards. Another grabs her tail. A dozen bodyguards grab Roxy too.

"I knew you were troublemakers, but I didn't know you were quitters!" says Tanuki. "I'm going to put you in my magic bag after all. It is a prison for troublemakers. And since you're quitters too, I know you won't try to get out!"

The bodyguards dump Fox into the bag. She yowls as she goes, but she knows that this is

# THE END

Go on to the next page.

Fox can't stand the idea of losing her umbrella. It's her most important possession! But if she doesn't do battle with Roxy, the big mean fox might never stop being a bully!

If Fox accepts Roxy's bet, TURN TO PAGE 9.

If Fox refuses to bet her umbrella, TURN TO PAGE 36.

Fox cuts through Roxy's ropes in a flash. "Get the kappa, Roxy!" Fox yells.

Roxy shrugs. "I don't really know how to fight," she admits. "I just threw tiny people around and acted scary."

Fox starts to yell at her, but no noise comes out. Everything goes dark. After a moment, she understands. The kappa has already popped her into its mouth! For Fox, this is clearly

**THE END**

Go on to the next page.

"The merchants gave me a silly-looking dress for the pageant, and when I put it on, they laughed at me! It hurt my feelings. I've been mean to them ever since!"

"That was a rotten thing for them to do," says Fox. She sets Roxy free. "Why don't we play a trick on them together?"

"I'd like that a lot, Fox!" says Roxy.

Roxy picks up her little cousin and gives her a big hug. "Thanks for looking out for me!"

## THE END

"Give me a turnip," says Fox. "I'll carve it to look like the monkey's nose. If I roll around on the ground, I'll be covered in dust. I'll be the same color as the statue!"

Fox rolls around in the dust and stuffs leaves into her shirt. Now she looks as big as the monkey!

Soon Tanuki returns and lays a biscuit down in front of Fox. He bows, and when he looks up, the biscuit is gone!

"Did I forget to give the statue a biscuit?" he asks. He sets down another. Again, he bows, and again, the biscuit disappears!

Suddenly Fox tosses off her disguise.

Tanuki laughs. "I can't beat that disguise!" he says. "You win!"

**THE END**

Go on to the next page. 

"There's an old fellow in gold robes!" says Fox. "There's also a young girl in the finest silk. She's probably a princess!"

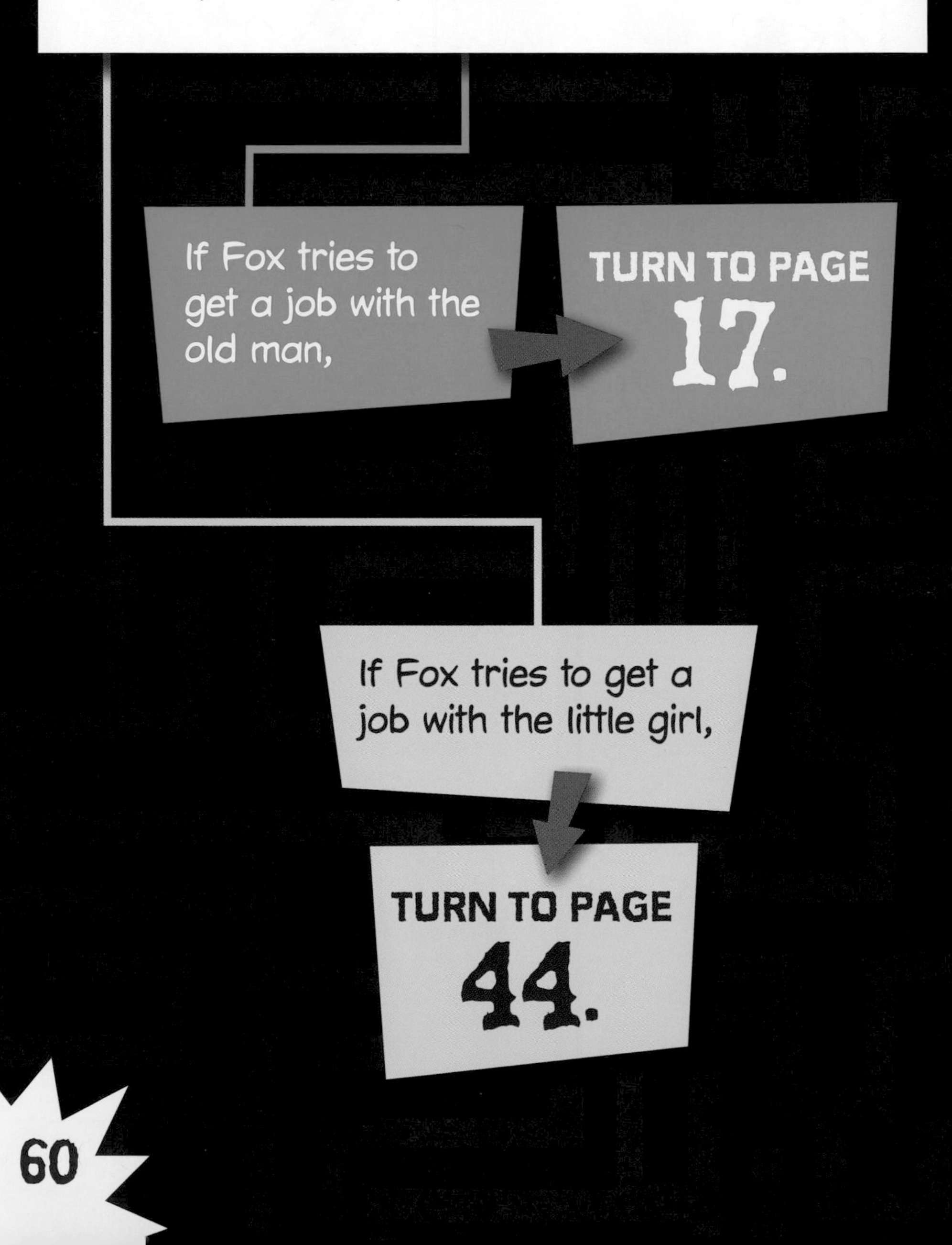

If Fox tries to get a job with the old man,

TURN TO PAGE 17.

If Fox tries to get a job with the little girl,

TURN TO PAGE 44.

"Here," says Fox, throwing the bag to Tanuki. "You know these guys better than I do. You should catch the biggest troublemaker first, and work your way down."

"That's exactly what I was planning to do!" says Tanuki.

Fox feels a sharp BONK on her head. Tanuki has hit her with his club. "You let all these crooks out," says Tanuki. "That means YOU'RE the biggest troublemaker of ALL!"

Tanuki throws Fox into the bag. For her, this is

## THE END

Go on to the next page.

Fox swims out until the water is up to her neck.

But Roxy doesn't get stuck. Roxy is so big, the water is only up to her knees, and she quickly catches Fox. Roxy lifts Fox out of the water.

"Looks like being quick and smart doesn't help that much after all!" growls Roxy. She pulls the umbrella off Fox's back. She tosses Fox out over the water.

Fox looks down and sees a shark with its mouth open, waiting for her to drop in for dinner. For Fox, this is

**THE END**

The character of **FOX** comes from the folktales of Japan. The stories are about many different foxes, which are called ***kitsune***.

In these stories, the foxes are often tricksters. They usually only trick people who are behaving foolishly. But kitsune are prideful creatures. They will trick anyone who claims to be more clever than foxes.

Kitsune are not only tricksters. Sometimes they try to protect people from harm or injustice. Sometimes they even fall in love with humans. And kitsune will do anything to repay someone who was kind to them.